DAVID MORTON

David Morton is a director, designer and playwright. He has created works for Lincoln Center, St. Ann's Warehouse, the New Victory Theater, Queensland Theatre, La Boite, Brisbane Festival, Sydney Opera House, Sydney Festival, Terrapin Puppet Company, Darwin Festival, Adelaide Festival Centre, The Garden of Unearthly Delights at the Adelaide Fringe, Metro Arts, Queensland Performing Arts Centre and the Brisbane Powerhouse.

David was named Best Director by the Matilda Awards in 2016 for *The Wider Earth*, and has been nominated for Helpmann Awards in writing and design in both 2016 and 2017, for *The Wider Earth* and *Laser Beak Man*. He holds a PhD from the Queensland University of Technology focusing on the contemporary use of puppetry for adult audiences.

David is a founding member and the Creative Director of the Dead Puppet Society.

David Morton

THE
WIDER EARTH

NICK HERN BOOKS

London

www.nickhernbooks.co.uk

A Nick Hern Book

The Wider Earth first published in Great Britain in 2018 as a paperback original by Nick Hern Books Limited, The Glasshouse, 49a Goldhawk Road, London W12 8QP

The Wider Earth copyright © 2018 David Morton

David Morton has asserted his moral rights to be identified as the author of this work

Cover image by Darren Bell
Production photography by Prudence Upton

Designed and typeset by Nick Hern Books, London
Printed in the UK by Mimeo Ltd, Huntingdon, Cambridgeshire PE29 6XX

A CIP catalogue record for this book is available from the British Library

ISBN   978 1 84842 813 3

Woodland
CARBON
www.woodlandcarbon.co.uk
NICK HERN BOOKS
Printed on Carbon Captured paper

Foreword
Professor Adrian Lister

I first encountered *The Wider Earth* having just completed
research on the *Beagle* voyage for my book, *Darwin's Fossils*.
I thought I knew the story pretty well, but as I read the script of
the play, the voyage, and Darwin's part in it, came vividly to
life for me in a new and powerful way. Darwin was in so many
ways stepping into the unknown – he had led a comfortable,
privileged life in England and had never been abroad, or at sea
for any duration. Now, aged only twenty-two, he found himself
sailing around the world, crammed with seventy-five sailors
into a small vessel of the British Navy.

The Darwin of the *Beagle* voyage was not the bearded sage of
popular imagery, but an energetic, enthusiastic young man with
a passion for natural history and geology. He had longed to visit
the tropics – the *Beagle* voyage was his dream come true and he
was determined to lose no opportunity for discovery and
adventure. Often when researching my book, I had been moved
by Darwin's prosaic descriptions of the natural wonders he had
witnessed, and this enchantment is wonderfully conveyed in the
visual imagery of *The Wider Earth*. The play forcefully shows
that the work of a great scientist is not a soulless enterprise of
dry calculation, but a personal, very human endeavour. We see
how the voyage affected Darwin's relations with his family, and
how he managed the brilliant but often difficult Captain
FitzRoy, who was his host.

It has been a tremendous pleasure for me to work with
playwright David Morton and Nick Paine of the Dead Puppet
Society as they created this script for the London production.
The diaries and letters of both Darwin and FitzRoy provide
a rich source of detail on the voyage, and on their personal
thoughts and feelings as events unfolded. David, Nick and
I discussed various key incidents and the development of

Darwin's thinking, and it has been exciting to see how these
have been skilfully incorporated into the narrative. Above all,
I have been impressed by the commitment of the writer and
producers to ensure the historical and scientific accuracy of the
script, without losing the sense of drama and adventure that
makes *The Wider Earth* such a remarkable and inspiring
theatrical experience.

*Professor Adrian Lister is Research Leader in Palaeontology at
the Natural History Museum, London, and Honorary Professor
in Genetics, Evolution and Environment at University College
London.*

Author's Note
David Morton

As a piece of visual theatre, the script for *The Wider Earth* intentionally makes use of ambitious stage directions to pose design challenges in the telling of the story. These are offered as a provocation for theatre artists to find inventive ways of incorporating visual forms into any production of the text, and should be read as a guide.

I encourage creative teams to find simple solutions to staging the visual elements, and to allow these extra considerations to promote play and innovation in their use of theatrical form. The story of *The Wider Earth* is about coming to terms with the complexity of the natural world, and I hope that future productions of the text embrace a similar commitment to generating moments of wonder.

Thanks

I would like to thank…

The cast and creatives who have dedicated their energy to bringing this story to life.

Nick Paine, who is the beating heart of our company.

Wesley Enoch, Sue Donnelly, Katherine Hoepper, Sam Strong, Amanda Jolly, and everyone at Queensland Theatre who championed the production.

Trish Wadley, who has made this version possible.

Clare Matterson who gave us a home at the Natural History Museum.

Professor Adrian Lister and Sebastian Born, for their input and guidance.

And Tony Brumpton, Justin Harrison, Aaron Barton and Sam Maher for being the perfect companions for the whole adventure.

D.M.

The Wider Earth was originally developed through The Lab
(Matt Acheson and Krissy Smith, Lab Directors) at St. Ann's
Warehouse in Brooklyn, New York City, USA, in 2014.

It was first presented by Queensland Theatre and Dead Puppet
Society at the Bille Brown Studio, Brisbane, Australia, on
9 July 2016. The cast was as follows (in alphabetical order):

REVEREND JOHN HENSLOW/ SIR JOHN HERSCHEL	Margi Brown Ash
VOICE OF OLD DARWIN	Robert Coleby
CHARLES DARWIN	Tom Conroy
EMMA WEDGWOOD	Lauren Jackson
JOHN CLEMENTS WICKHAM	Thomas Larkin
ROBERT DARWIN/ RICHARD MATTHEWS	David Lynch
JEMMY BUTTON	Jonty Martin
ROBERT FITZROY	Anthony Standish
POLLY	Anna Straker

Writer/Director/Co-Designer/ Puppet Designer	David Morton
Creative Producer/ Puppet Fabricator	Nicholas Paine
Co-Designer	Aaron Barton
Lighting Designer	David Walters
Co-Composers	Lior
	Tony Buchen
Sound Designer	Tony Brumpton
Projection Designer	Justin Harrison
Dramaturg	Louise Gough
Assistant Puppet Coach	Helen Stephens
Voice and Dialect Coach	Melissa Agnew
Illustrator and Puppet Arting	Anna Straker
Puppet Fabricator	Matthew Seery
Puppet Fabricator (Secondment)	Tia-Hanee Cleary

Stage Manager	Jodie Roche-Jones
Assistant Stage Manager/	Sam Maher
Sound Operator	

The production transferred to the Sydney Opera House, as part of the Sydney Festival, on 17 January 2018.

The Wider Earth received its European premiere in a purpose-built theatre in the Jerwood Gallery at the Natural History Museum, London, on 12 October 2018 (previews from 2 October). The cast was as follows (in alphabetical order):

REVEREND JOHN HENSLOW/ SIR JOHN HERSCHEL	Andrew Bridgmont
JEMMY BUTTON	Marcello Cruz
CHARLES DARWIN	Bradley Foster
ROBERT DARWIN/ RICHARD MATTHEWS	Ian Houghton
ROBERT FITZROY	Jack Parry-Jones
JOHN CLEMENTS WICKHAM/ ADAM SEDGWICK	Matt Tait
EMMA WEDGWOOD	Melissa Vaughan
Understudies	Rory Fairbairn
	Kim Scopes
Writer/Director/Co-Designer	David Morton
Creative Producer	Nicholas Paine
Co-Designer	Aaron Barton
Co-Composers	Lior
	Tony Buchen
Projection Designer	Justin Harrison
Sound Designer	Tony Brumpton
UK Lighting Designer	Lee Curran
Lighting Designer	David Walters
Puppet Design	Dead Puppet Society
Casting Director	Ellie Collyer-Bristow CDG
UK Dramaturg	Sebastian Born
Dramaturg	Louise Gough
Script Consultant	Professor Adrian Lister
Design Coordinator	Rebecca Brower
Technical Manager	Sam Maher
Company Stage Manager	Sophia Dalton

Assistant Stage Manager/ Book Cover	Karen Brown
Assistant Stage Manager	Kim Scopes
Lead Producer	Trish Wadley Productions
Creator and Producer	Dead Puppet Society
Co-Producer	Glass Half Full Productions
Associate Producer	Queensland Theatre

DEAD PUPPET SOCIETY (*Creator and Producer*)

Dead Puppet Society is a visual theatre and design company working across Australia and in New York City. Initially developed at St. Ann's Warehouse and Lincoln Centre, *The Wider Earth* premiered with Queensland Theatre in 2016 and transferred to the Sydney Opera House for Sydney Festival in 2018. Their most recent production, *Laser Beak Man* (with Brisbane Festival and La Boite in association with PowerArts), premiered in 2017 following a two-year residency at The New Victory Theater in New York City.

Prior to this, the Society created a suite of works with various companies in Brisbane before undertaking mentorship with Handspring Puppet Company (*War Horse*) in South Africa in 2013, and breaking into the international touring market with their critically acclaimed work *Argus* (Lincoln Center, Kravis Center Florida, Australian national tour). Previous works include *The Harbinger* (La Boite Theatre Company, Australian national tour), *The Timely Death of Victory Blott* (Metro Arts) and *Little Grey Wolf* (Brisbane Festival and Adelaide Fringe). The Society has received several awards from The Jim Henson Foundation for the creation of new work, and was awarded the Gold Matilda Award in 2017 for their body of work.

TRISH WADLEY PRODUCTIONS (*Lead Producer*)

Trish Wadley spent twenty years working internationally in media before moving to London theatre and has worked at the Bush Theatre and Tricycle Theatre.

As Executive Producer for Defibrillator: *A Lie of the Mind* (Southwark Playhouse); *Speech & Debate* (Trafalgar Studios); *Insignificance* (Langham Place, New York); *The Armour* (Langham, London); *The Hotel Plays* (Langham, London and Grange Hotel); *The One Day of the Year* and *Hard Feelings* (Finborough).

As producer: Olivier-nominated *The Red Lion* (Trafalgar Studios); *Fresh Lines* (Spring, Somerset House); *Burning Bridges* (Theatre503).

As co-producer: *My Night With Reg* (Apollo Theatre).

Trish is a Stage One Bursary recipient and director of The Uncertainty Principle. She is also a founder of The Australian & New Zealand Festival of Literature & Arts (FANZA).

GLASS HALF FULL PRODUCTIONS (*Co-Producer*)

Glass Half Full Productions is managed by Gareth Lake and founded by Gareth and Adam Blanshay. UK credits include *King Lear*, *Caroline, or Change*, *Glengarry Glen Ross*, *Daisy Pulls It Off*, *Oslo*, *Hamlet*, *Dreamgirls*, *Buried Child*, *Funny Girl*, *The Spoils*, *Doctor Faustus*, *Made in Dagenham*, *Sunny Afternoon*, *The Nether*, *Shrek* UK tour, *Dirty Rotten Scoundrels*, *I Can't Sing*, *Ghost Stories*, *1984*, *Ghosts*. Broadway credits include *Groundhog Day*, *Sunday in the Park with George*, *The Curious Incident of the Dog in the Night-time*, and the transfer from Shakespeare's Globe of *Twelfth Night/Richard III*. International credits include *Matilda* and *My Fair Lady* in Australia, and the international tour of the Blue Man Group.

QUEENSLAND THEATRE (*Associate Producer*)

Queensland Theatre is Australia's third largest theatre company, under the artistic direction of Sam Strong. For nearly fifty years, Queensland Theatre has enriched the cultural life of Australia by creating exceptional experiences that reach out to people of all generations across the state. Each year Queensland Theatre presents eight to ten mainstage productions in Brisbane, ranging from classics through to contemporary Australian and international stories. The company also tours extensively around Australia and occasionally, internationally. Running alongside the mainstage season are long-standing community-engagement initiatives: the Regional, Education and Youth, and Indigenous programs. Queensland Theatre has nurtured the careers of creative greats such as Geoffrey Rush, Bille Brown, Wesley Enoch and Deborah Mailman, and reflected Queensland back to itself by developing over one hundred new plays. Queensland Theatre is currently experiencing a surge in audiences, making it the fastest-growing theatre company in Australia.

Production photos from the 2018 Sydney Festival and Sydney Opera House presentation of The Wider Earth
Photos by Prudence Upton

THE WIDER EARTH

David Morton

Characters

CHARLES DARWIN, *a young man*
REVEREND JOHN HENSLOW, *his mentor. A botany professor from Cambridge*
ADAM SEDGWICK, *a geologist from Cambridge*
ROBERT DARWIN, *his father*
EMMA WEDGEWOOD, *his cousin. Later his wife*
ROBERT FITZROY, *the Captain of HMS* Beagle
JOHN WICKHAM, *the First Officer of HMS* Beagle
JEMMY BUTTON *from Tierra del Fuego, returning as a missionary*
RICHARD MATTHEWS, *another missionary*
JOHN HERSCHEL, *an astronomer and philosopher*

Creatures

Butterflies, a green iguana, fireflies, bioluminescent plankton, a southern right whale, an armadillo, a glyptodon, blue sharks, a shoal of fish, a marine iguana, a flightless cormorant, a sea-lion pup, a blue-footed booby, finches, a domed tortoise, a saddle-back tortoise, a platypus, a green sea turtle, arctic terns.

Locations

The Mount – *the Darwin estate, Shrewsbury, Shropshire*

Cambridge – *Henslow's rooms*

Maer Hall – *the Wedgewood estate, Maer, Staffordshire*

London – *the Admiralty Building, Whitehall*

Plymouth – *the Naval docks*

HMS *Beagle* – *a survey ship charting South America and circumnavigating the globe*

Tenerife – *an island in the Canary Archipelago*

St Jago – *an island in the Cape Verde Archipelago*

Bahia – *a dense rainforest in Brazil*

The Pampas – *grassy plains in Argentina*

The Southern Ocean – *a kelp forest*

Tierra del Fuego – *a bleak shoreline crowned with glaciers*

The Andes – *the peak of a mountain*

The Galápagos – *the rocky shore, the slopes of an extinct volcano*

Kaitaia Mission – *North Island, New Zealand*

Australia – *the banks of a small creek, Sydney*

Keeling Island – *a coral lagoon in the Indian Ocean*

Cape Town – *a house under Table Mountain, South Africa*

1.

Beginning at the End

The voice of a young CHILD *breaks into the darkness.*

CHILD (*voice-over*). In the beginning, God created the heaven and the earth. The earth was without form, and darkness covered the face of the deep. Until God said, let there be light.

A glowing sphere appears.

And there was light.

The voice slowly matures, reading with increasing pace and running over itself. It is joined by others, until it becomes a cacophony of words.

The glowing light slowly becomes the forming Earth.

VOICES (*voice-over*). On the second day, the waters above were separated from the water below, enclosing the earth.

On the third day, the waters ran together and dry land appeared. God caused the earth to bud with herbs and plants with seeds and fruits, and the tree of knowledge of good and evil.

On the fourth day the sun, the moon and the rest of the stars were created.

On the fifth day fish and flying birds were created and commanded to multiply and fill the sea and earth.

On the sixth day creatures of the land were created.

Last of all was man crafted after the image of God, and woman from his rib. They were given dominion over all living creatures.

On the seventh day, God rested and beheld all that he had made.

It was perfect, as no sin had yet entered creation.

At the end of the first week of the world, God brought the newly created couple into the Garden of Eden, and charged them not to eat of the tree of knowledge of good and evil.

The spinning globe is complete and rests into its orbit.

The chorus of voices falls away to one.

CHARLES (*voice-over*). This beginning of all time, according to the chronology recorded in the Holy Bible, happened four thousand and four years before the birth of Christ, less than six thousand years from the current day.

The globe spins and grows until it reveals Shrewsbury, a small village in Shropshire.

EMMA WEDGEWOOD *walks towards The Mount, the home of the Darwin family, flicking through a book loosely wrapped in brown paper.*

CHARLES DARWIN *approaches.*

EMMA. Charles?

CHARLES. I'm home.

EMMA. I trust the voyage was everything you hoped for.

CHARLES. Everything and more.

EMMA. You've been gone such a long time.

CHARLES. Five years.

EMMA. You told me it would be two.

CHARLES. I know.

A breath.

EMMA. I received a proposal, Mr Darwin.

CHARLES. Did you reject it?

EMMA. Not yet.

CHARLES. Is he worthy of you?

EMMA. I certainly hope so.

CHARLES. How can you not be sure?

EMMA. He is a stranger to me.

CHARLES. Then do not accept his hand.

EMMA. The world didn't sit still while you were gone,
    Mr Darwin.

CHARLES. Apparently not.

EMMA. How is it you can be away for so long, yet return so
    thoroughly unchanged?

CHARLES. Do you not wish to hear what I've seen?

EMMA. I've not waited five years to find out that you're still
    a lost boy.

CHARLES. Let me tell you why you're wrong.

EMMA. I don't have the patience for a thousand of your
    thoughts any more.

CHARLES. Then hear just one. Though to be fair, it does take
    a good deal of explaining.

EMMA. This had better be a good story, Charles Darwin.

CHARLES. It's rather more than just that.

The globe spins back in time.

Glowing lines form words – 'THE WIDER EARTH'.

The letters are blown away like sand.

2.

Leaving Cambridge

CHARLES *lies in the grounds of Cambridge reading Humboldt.*

Movement on the ground catches his eye.

CHARLES. Beetles!

He takes a beetle in his hands, but can't open the specimen jar so throws them into his mouth.

REVEREND JOHN HENSLOW *arrives.*

HENSLOW. Charles Darwin! Why is it that the rest of the college is able to attend morning lectures, and yet I find you here enjoying the sunshine?

CHARLES *chokes on the beetle.*

Good Lord, boy. Are you all right?

CHARLES. I'm fine, Professor.

HENSLOW. What on earth was that?

CHARLES. A beetle, sir.

HENSLOW. In your mouth?

CHARLES. My hands were full.

HENSLOW. Give me strength.

CHARLES. It was a crucifix ground beetle, sir. Did you see where it went?

HENSLOW. I'd say it's long gone by now.

CHARLES. I've not found one before.

HENSLOW. You might have passed your examinations, Charles, but they don't just hand out Bachelor Degrees.

CHARLES. I only needed two more terms of residence to graduate.

HENSLOW. Enjoying mornings in the sun hardly qualifies, unorthodox beetle collecting or not.

A breath.

CHARLES. Did you sign for my attendance at the lecture?

HENSLOW. Why would I do that?

CHARLES. Oh, come on, Henslow.

HENSLOW. Of course I did, my boy.

CHARLES. Thank you, sir.

A breath.

I was reading Humboldt.

HENSLOW. There's the culprit.

CHARLES. If you wanted me to attend lectures I don't know why you gave me his book, sir.

HENSLOW. You'll have to excuse me for hoping you might be able to balance your studies with your daydreaming.

CHARLES. His descriptions of Tenerife make me feel as if I'm wandering the tropics. Do you think we'll still be able to make a trip there before the new term?

HENSLOW. I've asked around. There's some interest, but I wouldn't hold your breath, Charles.

CHARLES. My father's convinced himself I should start my theology training.

HENSLOW. Then I suppose we'll be seeing you next term?

CHARLES. I suppose you will.

HENSLOW. Is that really so bad?

CHARLES. When I finish at Christ's, I'll be shipped off to some parish.

HENSLOW. There are worse pursuits, my boy.

CHARLES. Priests don't travel the world though, do they, sir?

HENSLOW. Listen, Tenerife or not, Professor Sedgwick is leading a geological survey to Wales over the summer. You're welcome to join him.

CHARLES. What's the point?

HENSLOW. Don't be sour, Charles. It doesn't suit you.

CHARLES. All that's left in this country are old rocks.

The map follows the road from Cambridge to Wales.

3.

Geologising

CHARLES *and* ADAM SEDGWICK *undertake the survey in Wales.*

SEDGWICK. Anything?

CHARLES. No, sir. Why do we have to find this sandstone?

SEDGWICK. So I can refute the dangerous new thinking of Charles Lyell and his lot that the features of the earth were the result of gradual change.

CHARLES. Why is that so important?

SEDGWICK. Because, young man, the earth is static and wrought in single catastrophic moments of upheaval.

A breath.

CHARLES. Back home in Shrewsbury, just outside town, I found the fossil of a marine shell in a gravel pit on the top of a ridge.

SEDGWICK. And what can you deduce from that?

CHARLES. The whole area used to be under the ocean.

SEDGWICK. Try again.

CHARLES. It must have been left behind after some great flood.

SEDGWICK. There's a far easier explanation.

CHARLES. What's that?

SEDGWICK. Somebody dropped it there.

CHARLES. Isn't that rather unimaginative?

SEDGWICK. Don't be afraid of the simple answer that's staring you in the face.

A breath.

CHARLES. There's also a boulder that people in the village call the bell stone.

SEDGWICK. And why is this boulder worthy of discussion?

CHARLES. It's a granite boulder. But there's nothing like it nearby. Mr Cotton told me the world would come to an end before anyone ever worked out how the bell stone came to be in Shrewsbury.

SEDGWICK. And who's Mr Cotton?

CHARLES. A geologist in town.

SEDGWICK. I've not heard of him.

CHARLES. He's a baker, really.

SEDGWICK. Meaning no disrespect to Mr Cotton and his wisdom, but he needn't wait to the end of time if he could read what was right before his eyes.

CHARLES. You're right. Someone probably dropped it there.

A breath.

Or perhaps it was pushed all the way to Shrewsbury during a great upheaval in the past.

SEDGWICK. We might just make a geologist of you yet, Mr Darwin.

CHARLES. And I might work out how a shell came to be on top of a ridge.

SEDGWICK. Come on. We'll find this sandstone if it takes us as far as Anglesea.

The map pulls back and is shaded and annotated with notes as to Welsh geology.

4.

The Letter

ROBERT DARWIN *watches as* CHARLES *approaches The Mount.*

ROBERT. Charles?

CHARLES. Hello, Father.

ROBERT. Welcome home, son.

>   ROBERT *produces an envelope.*

>   A letter came for you. From a Reverend Henslow.

CHARLES. When did it arrive?

ROBERT. A couple of weeks ago. Who is he, Charles?

CHARLES. A botany professor from Cambridge.

>   CHARLES *reads.*

>   Henslow says there's no chance of a trip to Tenerife this summer.

ROBERT. That's for the best.

CHARLES. Wait. There's a voyage to the Americas. A real one. With the Navy. Henslow was invited to be the naturalist, but he can't be gone for two years. He put my name forward in his place. I have a meeting with the Captain!

>   *A breath.*

ROBERT. Tell me something, Charles. How long do you presume I should support your idle pleasures?

CHARLES. Father, this is hardly an idle pleasure.

ROBERT. All you care for is dogs and guns and rat-catching.

CHARLES. I just completed my degree.

ROBERT. You scraped through, without honours.

CHARLES. I had the finest beetle collection in the college.

ROBERT. Beetles!? You were supposed to be studying Classics.

CHARLES. This is my chance for an adventure, just like Humboldt and the other great naturalists.

ROBERT. It's just another wild scheme, another obstacle to you taking your life seriously. Do you not see the damage it would do your reputation as a clergyman?

CHARLES. I'm not a member of the clergy, Father.

ROBERT. Not yet. But you're returning to Christ's to complete your theology training whether you like it or not.

CHARLES. An opportunity like this won't come around again.

ROBERT. After all these years, not to mention expense, I've finally managed to find you a worthwhile pursuit. You're a fool if you think I'll let it slip by.

CHARLES. How is a voyage not worthwhile?

ROBERT. The Navy? God help me, Charles, there's no station on this earth that suits you less.

CHARLES. Then give me a chance to prove myself.

ROBERT. It is beyond you.

CHARLES. Not if you'll pay my board.

ROBERT. It's not money you are lacking. I forbid you to sail on that boat.

A breath.

Where are you going?

CHARLES. Maer Hall.

ROBERT. Ask Miss Wedgwood to knock some sense into you. Tell me, when exactly does she become Mrs Darwin on your terms?

CHARLES. When she resigns herself to having an unreasonable oaf as a father-in-law.

ROBERT. Unreasonable? Honestly, Charles, you find me one sensible man who thinks this voyage is a good idea and I'll reconsider. But I can promise you something – he doesn't exist.

CHARLES turns to leave as The Mount gives way to Maer Hall.

5.

An Unfortunate Taste for Beetles

CHARLES *approaches Maer Hall, estate of the Wedgwood family, where he meets* EMMA.

EMMA. Charlie! I wasn't expecting you today.

CHARLES. Neither was I.

EMMA. The hunt doesn't begin until tomorrow.

CHARLES. Better early than never.

EMMA. When have you ever missed the chance for a day of shooting?

He examines a medallion hanging on a string around her neck.

CHARLES. What's this?

EMMA. Father's planning a protest outside Parliament.

CHARLES. And what's his cause this time?

EMMA. The abolishment of slavery, across the entire empire. Our pottery works has made medallions for people to show their support.

CHARLES. The old trolls in the House of Lords are hardly going to change their minds over trinkets.

EMMA. If we all stand together they'll have no choice. Every man deserves freedom, regardless of the part they play.

CHARLES. Try telling that to my father.

EMMA. You are hardly a slave, Mr Darwin.

CHARLES. I can't imagine it could be much worse.

EMMA. Oh, please.

A breath.

You fought with him again, didn't you?

CHARLES. He treats me like some sort of fool.

EMMA. And how did you bait him this time?

CHARLES. He wants me to start my theology training in the new term.

EMMA. That's wonderful news.

CHARLES. Is it?

EMMA. Something to be proud of.

A breath.

CHARLES. I received a letter.

EMMA. A good many people receive letters, Charles.

CHARLES. Not like this one they don't.

She reads.

EMMA. You didn't think to accept this, did you?

CHARLES. Of course I did.

EMMA. God has already given your life purpose. Why stray from that path of faith?

CHARLES. Because it's not what I want.

EMMA. You'd rather throw away two years of your life to go and play at some silly voyage?

CHARLES. You sound just like my father.

EMMA. He's been so patient with you. We all have. You can't just keep skipping from one flight of fancy to the next without a thought for the consequences.

CHARLES. This is different. There might be a future in it.

EMMA. In what? Your unfortunate taste for beetles?

CHARLES. If I don't take this opportunity I'll always wonder what could have been.

EMMA. No you won't. You'll finish your training. Settle down in a parish. Have a family. A wife.

CHARLES. Not yet. I'm not ready.

EMMA. Apparently not.

A breath.

CHARLES. You believe I could make something more of myself, don't you?

EMMA. Of course I do.

CHARLES. This is the means for it. But only the opinion of a sensible man means anything to my father.

EMMA. Does it just?

Maer Hall spins back to The Mount.

6.

A Chance at Freedom

Back at The Mount, CHARLES *presents a letter to his father as* EMMA *stands nearby.*

ROBERT. What's this?

CHARLES. From Uncle Josiah.

> ROBERT *tears the envelope open.*

ROBERT. A man of enlarged curiosity? He's saying you're odd.

CHARLES. And that an opportunity like this could be just what I need to find my place in the world.

> *A breath.*

ROBERT. Do you agree with your father?

EMMA. There's no point keeping him here if his mind's still wandering.

CHARLES. Only a handful of men ever get this chance, Father.

ROBERT. Are these your uncle's words or yours?

CHARLES. He is a sensible man, don't you think?

ROBERT. You're a clever one, I'll give you that.

CHARLES. And will you give your consent?

ROBERT. Yes.

> *A breath.*

On the condition that when you return, you either join the clergy, or you make your own way in this world.

CHARLES. I won't disappoint you.

ROBERT. Don't do anything foolish, Charles.

> ROBERT *leaves.*

CHARLES. Thank you, Em.

EMMA. You're indebted to me for this, you know.

CHARLES. I thought you'd done it for the greater good.

EMMA. What's that supposed to mean?

CHARLES. Does the world really need another miserable priest?

The Mount spins away and the map traces the journey to London.

7.

The Captain

In the Admiralty Building in London, Captain ROBERT FITZROY *looks through paperwork with his First Officer, Lieutenant* JOHN WICKHAM.

FITZROY. Have the chronometers arrived, Lieutenant?

WICKHAM. Not yet, Captain.

FITZROY. Have the order forwarded straight to Plymouth.

WICKHAM. Yes, sir.

CHARLES *enters.*

Can I help you?

CHARLES. I'm looking for Robert FitzRoy.

WICKHAM. What's your business with him?

CHARLES. He sought a naturalist for his voyage.

FITZROY. You're late, Mr Darwin.

CHARLES. I was on a field trip in Wales. You're FitzRoy?

FITZROY. Captain, Mr Darwin. Or sir at the very least.

CHARLES. Sorry, sir.

FITZROY. Do you know the purpose of the voyage?

CHARLES. You sail to the Americas.

FITZROY. Don't confuse the destination with the purpose. We seek out the perilous waters of South America so we might draw a chart to give other vessels safe passage. Then we'll carry a chain of chronometric measurements back around the far side of the world. A full circumnavigation.

CHARLES. I've always dreamt of an adventure just like that, sir. I've never been on a boat.

A breath.

FITZROY. The *Beagle* is a ship, Mr Darwin. A ten-gun brig sloop, if you've a fancy for detail.

CHARLES. I do, sir.

FITZROY. I haven't spent the better part of the last year and a small fortune in refitting to have her called a boat.

CHARLES. No. Sorry.

FITZROY. In addition to a naturalist I had hoped for a companion for the voyage. You are at least capable of intelligent conversation I assume?

CHARLES. Yes, sir. I think so, sir.

FITZROY. This meeting gives absolutely no indication.

CHARLES. No.

A breath.

FITZROY. Your training is in the Classics? Yes?

CHARLES. I pursued other interests outside of my studies, sir. Entomology, some botany.

FITZROY. On the *Beagle*'s last voyage I was struck by the varied geology we encountered, and what an opportunity it would present for some young naturalist to make their mark.

CHARLES. I could do that, sir.

FITZROY. Do what exactly, Mr Darwin?

CHARLES. Make a mark.

FITZROY. You're going to have to be more specific.

CHARLES. I've a growing interest in geology, that's why I was in Wales.

FITZROY. And how exactly does that qualify you?

CHARLES. You won't find anyone who wants this more, sir.

FITZROY. Very good. I dare say in any other world you would have been a suitable candidate for the position.

CHARLES. Why not in this world?

FITZROY. You were so delayed in your arrival that I've already offered it elsewhere.

CHARLES. It's already been filled?

FITZROY. I hope you won't begrudge me taking up your time. Reverend Henslow spoke very highly of you. It is a pleasure to have met you, Mr Darwin.

CHARLES. I wish you the best for your voyage, sir.

The offices fade away as the map travels to Cambridge.

8.

The Makings of a Naturalist

HENSLOW *sits in his rooms in Cambridge. There is a knock on the door.*

HENSLOW. Come.

    CHARLES *enters.*

    Charles Darwin.

CHARLES. Evening, Professor.

HENSLOW. Who's going to show up unannounced when you've gone halfway around the world?

CHARLES. You needn't worry about that, sir.

HENSLOW. FitzRoy did offer you the position, didn't he?

CHARLES. I was too late.

    A breath.

    My father was right. There was nothing real to be gained by it.

HENSLOW. There was everything to be gained.

CHARLES. This whole business of voyaging is just a silly dream.

    A breath.

    Professor?

HENSLOW. Listen to me, Charles. I have an old friend living in Cape Town, Sir John Herschel. He works at capturing light on glass so that he can record the world just as we see it – to paint a picture with light.

CHARLES. That's not possible.

HENSLOW. Not yet it isn't. But when he solves the riddle of the picture do you think he'll be remembered as a silly dreamer?

CHARLES. I suppose not.

HENSLOW. He'll be a hero!

CHARLES. And when he fails?

HENSLOW. He will have spent his life doing something that he loved. Nothing that's meaningful in this world comes easy, Charles.

CHARLES. I know that.

HENSLOW. Then I think you'd better open this.

He hands CHARLES *a letter.*

CHARLES. It's from the Admiralty.

HENSLOW. Arrived just before you.

CHARLES *opens it and reads.*

Well?

CHARLES. It's mine. The position's mine.

HENSLOW. I knew it.

CHARLES. I'm going to see Tenerife!

HENSLOW. You'll see a good deal more than that, my boy.

A breath.

CHARLES. Professor, I feel so thoroughly unworthy of all of this.

HENSLOW. You've open eyes and an open mind. There's no one better suited.

CHARLES. That doesn't make me feel better.

HENSLOW. If you send a trained naturalist into the field, every find will reassure him of what he already thinks he knows. But send a young man who knows nothing and there's no telling what he might find. Take this.

HENSLOW *gives* CHARLES *an empty journal.*

CHARLES. A journal?

HENSLOW. Small observations, rigorously noted. That's our method, Charles, you know it already. I don't expect you'll know what you've found, but at least you'll have notes for when you work it all out.

CHARLES. Work what out, sir?

HENSLOW. Only heaven knows what that might be, my young friend. One more thing.

CHARLES. Your microscope. I can't accept this, Professor.

HENSLOW. Charles, I'm quite sick of hearing what you cannot do. I have given it to you. I will not take it back.

CHARLES. It's a fine gift.

HENSLOW. Suitable for a naturalist on his grand adventure, I should think.

CHARLES. You're not going to let me refuse you, are you?

HENSLOW. Not in this life, nor the next. Now time is short, and you need supplies.

HENSLOW *starts to write a list*.

Twelve shirts in one canvas bag.

CHARLES *packs the items as they come together*.

One pair slippers. One pair light walking boots. One geological hammer. One geological compass.

CHARLES. All packed, sir.

More and more packages are added.

HENSLOW. One plain compass. One telescope. One writing set. And one pencil case.

CHARLES *adds these to his trunk*.

CHARLES. What's next?

HENSLOW. Five sympisometers!

CHARLES. Five what?

HENSLOW. For measuring altitude. One, two, three, four and five.

CHARLES *packs these away too*.

Three mountain barometers, air pressure. One clinometer, angle of slope. One hygrometer, humidity.

HENSLOW *hands* CHARLES *the final items*.

One microscope, single lens. And one journal for notes.

CHARLES. Thank you, sir.

They embrace.

HENSLOW. Don't be blinded by thoughts of impressive achievements, my young friend. It's the small things that change the world. Remember that.

CHARLES. What will I do without you, Professor?

HENSLOW. Amazing things, Charles Darwin, amazing things.

The map charts the journey back to Shrewsbury.

9.

Not Your Butterfly

Back at The Mount.

CHARLES. Will you keep an eye on my father?

EMMA. Until your return.

CHARLES. I'll be home before you know it.

EMMA. Hold this.

She hands CHARLES *his coat while she ties his neck cloth*.

CHARLES. I thought, maybe, our parting might be easier if you would consent to be my wife?

EMMA. Really, Charles?

CHARLES. I've made a list of the pros and cons and it seems like the most logical step to take.

EMMA. I'm not a butterfly to be pinned in your collection. Turn around.

She helps him with his coat.

CHARLES. I thought that was what you wanted.

EMMA. Just make your time count for something, for both our sakes.

CHARLES. And you'll accept my proposal when I return?

EMMA. That depends entirely on who we've become.

A breath.

CHARLES. How do I look?

EMMA. You certainly look the part.

A breath.

CHARLES. Nothing need change while I'm gone.

EMMA. Perhaps it would be better if it did. You might just grow up, Mr Darwin.

The Mount gives way to the map, which traces the journey to Plymouth.

10.

The *Beagle*

CHARLES *boards the* Beagle *as preparations are made for departure.*

FITZROY. Mr Darwin! How do you find HMS *Beagle*?

CHARLES. Amazing, sir.

FITZROY. I trust she lives up to your expectations.

CHARLES. Not bad, for a boat.

FITZROY. This way. You remember Lieutenant John Wickham.

WICKHAM. What are you, Mr Darwin, brave or mad?

CHARLES. Quite definitely mad.

WICKHAM. You're in good company then.

> CHARLES *follows* FITZROY *to the chart room.*

FITZROY. Cramped, but all we can afford you. There's a separate hold for any specimens you think worthy of the space.

CHARLES. Thank you, sir.

FITZROY. I have something for you.

> *He hands* CHARLES *a book.*

CHARLES. *Principles of Geology.* Charles Lyell.

FITZROY. The leading young geologist of our age. Sounds like he's causing quite the stir.

CHARLES. I can read it.

FITZROY. Can you just?

CHARLES. You didn't have to do this, sir.

FITZROY. Welcome aboard, Mr Darwin.

> RICHARD MATTHEWS *and* JEMMY BUTTON *come aboard.*

MATTHEWS. Captain FitzRoy!

FITZROY. Matthews.

MATTHEWS. Your *Beagle* is an impressive vessel for a first command, I must say.

CHARLES. This is your first command?

FITZROY. The first I've taken out from port. On the last voyage I only brought her home.

They join the newcomers on deck.

Richard Matthews and Jemmy Button here sail with us to establish a Christian mission in Tierra del Fuego. Mr Darwin is our naturalist.

CHARLES. You didn't mention a Christian mission before.

MATTHEWS. FitzRoy might tell you this whole undertaking is about surveying and the making of a map. There's more to it than that.

FITZROY. Not in the eyes of the Admiralty. They didn't see the worth in the Christian mission. But the *Beagle*'s previous captain left the southern charts unfinished. God rest his soul.

CHARLES. What happened to him, sir?

FITZROY. I'll not speak of it today, here at the start of so many good things.

MATTHEWS. You bring light to this world in more ways than one, my old friend.

FITZROY. We'll have you home in a few short months, Mr Button, good to my word.

JEMMY. Thank you, sir.

CHARLES. Are you from Tierra del Fuego?

JEMMY. Yes, sir.

CHARLES. You're such a long way from home.

JEMMY. Soon that will be you, Mr Darwin.

CHARLES. Yes, I suppose it will.

WICKHAM. We have the wind, Captain!

FITZROY. Very good. Have the boatswain call the crew to stations and cast us off. She may not have the gun power she once did but I would have a salute fired.

WICKHAM. I'll see to it.

FITZROY. You have the deck, Mr Wickham.

WICKHAM. Thank you, sir. Boatswain!

FITZROY. Matthews, would you lead us in a prayer?

MATTHEWS. I would be honoured, sir.

FITZROY. For king and country, gentlemen. And God Almighty.

The boatswain's whistle sounds.

MATTHEWS. Oh creator past all telling, you have appointed the treasures of your wisdom, and so beautifully set out all parts of the universe.

The Beagle *pulls away from the dock and the cannons fire.*

You we call the true fount of wisdom, the noble origin of all things.

The cannons fire again. CHARLES *marvels at the movement of the ship as she cuts through the waves.*

Shed the darkness of mind in which we were born, make us keen to understand, quick to learn, delicate to interpret, and ready to speak.

They fire again.

Guide on our going forward, lead home our going forth. You are true and rule forever. In the name of Jesus Christ our Lord. Amen.

ALL. Amen.

The Beagle *turns, time passes.*

CHARLES *suffers from seasickness in his cabin as the map charts the journey to Tenerife.*

11.

Quarantine

CHARLES *wakes in his cabin and realises that the* Beagle *is at anchor.*

CHARLES. Where are we?

WICKHAM. Tenerife.

CHARLES. We're already there?

WICKHAM. You've been in your cabin for weeks.

CHARLES *climbs to get a better look.*

CHARLES. How soon can I go ashore?

WICKHAM. There was an outbreak of cholera in England. We'd have wait out twelve days in quarantine before they'll grant us leave to make land.

CHARLES. How am I supposed to pass twelve days with the island so close?

WICKHAM. You won't have to. We're continuing south to Cape Verde.

CHARLES. Surely we can't have come all this way to miss Tenerife. Captain?

FITZROY. We've no business here. Our late departure from England has already put us behind.

CHARLES. I have to set foot on that island, sir.

FITZROY. Or what, Mr Darwin? I'll not delay us further so you can live out some fantasy.

CHARLES. What's a few extra days?

FITZROY. This voyage is not your pleasure cruise. You'd do well to remember it. Weigh anchor.

WICKHAM. All hands on deck.

The boatswain's whistle sounds.

There'll be plenty more islands, Mr Darwin.

CHARLES. Not like that one there won't.

The boatswain's whistle sounds as CHARLES *watches
Tenerife recede into the distance.*

12.

Uniformitarianism

CHARLES *takes Lyell's book from the shelf and returns to the
deck to read as the* Beagle *moves on. The map charts the
journey to Cape Verde.*

CHARLES. A sketch of the progress of geology is the history of
a constant and violent struggle between new opinions and
ancient doctrines. In attempting to explain geological
creation the bias has always been placed on the catastrophic
suddenness and violence of changes, rather than framing
theories in accordance with the ongoing processes of nature.

*The world spins, and the ship gives way to the island of
St Jago.*

In the pursuit of geological truth I offer the following
provocation: that the action of the present is the key to the past.

On the shore of St Jago, CHARLES *stands at the top of
a low rise and marvels at the scene before him.*

*He examines a white band in the exposed strata of a cliff
side.*

13.

Lofty Thoughts for Lofty Men

The Beagle *continues the journey south.*

FITZROY. I see you've been reading Lyell's book?

CHARLES. I have, sir.

FITZROY. And how do you find it?

CHARLES. Unlike anything I've ever read.

FITZROY. It's unlike anything ever written.

MATTHEWS. What is this book?

CHARLES. It outlines a theory that gradual geological
    processes might have led to the current shape of the earth.

MATTHEWS. That contradicts scripture.

CHARLES. It contradicts more than that.

FITZROY. You disagree with him?

CHARLES. Not entirely, no. In St Jago there was a white layer
    of shells in the cliff sides far above sea level.

FITZROY. And what do you make of that?

CHARLES. A month ago I would have told you how a great
    torrent of water could have carved out the valleys of the
    island and left sediment in its wake. Now I'm not so sure.
    It's almost like the ground had risen.

MATTHEWS. Dangerous territory, my friend.

CHARLES. I don't agree with all Lyell has to say, but he
    reasons everything with such clarity, it's hard not to see the
    world through his eyes.

A breath.

I think you're right, sir. There's definitely a book in the
geology we encounter.

CHARLES *begins to make the first notes in his gently
glowing journal as the* Beagle *continues her journey south.*

14.

Nature's Cathedral

In Bahia, Brazil, CHARLES *enters a tropical rainforest for the first time.*

He is the vision of a naturalist, with his butterfly net, and crate for specimens.

He catches a butterfly and bottles it.

CHARLES *prepares to move on.*

He climbs a buttress to look out over the canopy.

As he returns to the ground he disturbs a swarm of butterflies.

An iguana appears.

CHARLES *teases it.*

The iguana runs away.

CHARLES *coaxes it back with food.*

He collects his journal.

Night falls around him and fireflies come out.

CHARLES *adds notes to his journal.*

Light rain builds into a thunderstorm.

The rainforest melts away.

15.

The Benefits of Slavery

CHARLES *and* WICKHAM *stand on the deck as preparations are made for the* Beagle *to depart.*

CHARLES. I'd never imagined there were so many different forms of life in all the world, let alone one forest. You couldn't take a step without stumbling upon something new.

WICKHAM. A successful excursion then.

CHARLES. Without a doubt. Though I never want to visit a slave country again.

WICKHAM. It is a reality for many in the new world, Mr Darwin.

CHARLES. In England, such atrocities seem so distant. One woman near my camp kept a screw clamp to crush the thumbs of her slaves.

FITZROY. Measures must be taken to keep them under control.

CHARLES. Surely that cannot justify such cruelty.

FITZROY. The strength of the British Empire is built on the backs of owned men. Whether you agree with it or not, we all benefit from slavery.

CHARLES. I heard of families being separated and any number of other things that make the heart sick.

FITZROY. You speak too freely for someone with no knowledge on the subject.

CHARLES. I know it would be a proud thing for England to be the first European country to abolish it completely.

FITZROY. And what would that achieve?

CHARLES. The freedom of every man and woman in the empire.

FITZROY. Rubbish, they do not want it.

CHARLES. How can you possibly say such a thing?

FITZROY. I once visited a man who called up his slaves and asked if they wanted to be free. All answered no. Every last one of them.

CHARLES. That means nothing in the presence of their master.

FITZROY. You disrespect me by your argument.

CHARLES. That's not my intention.

FITZROY. Yet it's the result.

WICKHAM. He meant no offence, sir.

FITZROY. Fight your own battles, Lieutenant. Jemmy!

JEMMY. Yes, Captain?

FITZROY. Mr Darwin here takes me for a liar. He seems to think it cruel to bring a man under the guiding hand of the empire. What do you think, Jemmy?

CHARLES. Sir, this really isn't necessary.

FITZROY. Let him speak!

JEMMY. It is a mercy, Captain. My life before was very hard. I stole, but you forgave.

FITZROY. You are not a slave, Jemmy. Yet maybe he still thinks you would only say what I wish to hear?

JEMMY. I live in the light of Christ. I'll save my people just the same.

FITZROY. Spoken like a gentleman who knows his place in the order of things. Wouldn't you agree, Mr Darwin?

CHARLES. Yes, sir.

FITZROY. Then the matter is settled. Thank you, Jemmy.

A breath.

What else can you tell me of the mighty rainforest?

CHARLES. The plants and animals were all very different to anything I've seen at home.

FITZROY. You're telling me the creatures were different to those of Europe?

CHARLES. Yes, sir, but –

FITZROY. Our naturalist! What a keen eye he has.

CHARLES. Look at this, sir.

FITZROY. A lizard?

CHARLES. An iguana.

FITZROY. What did you say?

CHARLES. It's not just a lizard.

FITZROY. You watch your tone or I'll have you shipped back to England. Clear this deck.

As the crew scatter, CHARLES *catches a moment with* JEMMY.

CHARLES. I hope I didn't offend you, Mr Button.

JEMMY. You only try to make your way.

CHARLES. Do you really agree with the Captain?

JEMMY. What we believe does not matter. You must do what you need to survive.

CHARLES *makes his way to his cabin as the* Beagle *cuts through a darkening sea.*

16.

Wonder and the Sum of its Parts

In the late evening, MATTHEWS *comes to* CHARLES *as he prepares his butterfly specimens.*

MATTHEWS. Slavery is a terrible business.

CHARLES. There was nothing to be gained by pressing the point with him.

MATTHEWS. Sometimes it speaks louder to say nothing at all.

CHARLES. I know.

MATTHEWS. These are very beautiful.

CHARLES. Back home I would hope that each day might greet me with some small discovery. Bahia was beyond anything I'd ever imagined. That forest made you feel there was more to a man than the breath in your body.

MATTHEWS. A noble sentiment.

CHARLES. It was like a cathedral for the god of nature. Yet I can't fathom the cruelty of it all. The slaves are one matter. I also found a wasp, that lays its eggs in a caterpillar so when its offspring hatch they eat the poor grub alive. Such suffering in such majesty. It seems a contradiction.

MATTHEWS. One cannot hope to study the design of the creator and think to understand it right away.

CHARLES. I couldn't capture the grandeur of the place. All I have are small finds.

The Beagle*'s wake begins to glow.*

MATTHEWS. Charles. There's something in the water.

CHARLES *climbs to get a better view.*

CHARLES. Pass me that bucket.

He collects the glowing seawater.

MATTHEWS. What in God's name is it?

CHARLES. I have no idea.

He places a drop of the water onto his microscope.

Incredible.

MATTHEWS. What do you see?

CHARLES. Hundreds of tiny creatures.

CHARLES *marvels at the wake the* Beagle *carves through the ocean.*

So much beauty for so little purpose.

MATTHEWS. Perhaps it's a lesson, Charles.

CHARLES. Even the greatest wonder is just the sum of tiny parts.

Below the waves, a southern right whale sings as it passes through the depths, leaving a glowing blue trail in its wake.

It breaches and spouts as it charts the Beagle*'s journey south.*

17.

The Southern Charts

CHARLES *works on the deck of the* Beagle *as the crew begin the process of surveying.*

FITZROY. Mr Darwin. A moment if you'd be so kind.

CHARLES. Yes, sir.

FITZROY. I owe you an explanation.

CHARLES. It wasn't my place to argue with you.

FITZROY. No, yet you obviously believe in the sanctity of each life. As do I. There is an argument that slavery civilises a man.

CHARLES. That's rather extreme, sir.

FITZROY. When you are confronted by the image of an
    untamed man, perhaps you will understand. It is a shock that
    one created in the image of God could have sunk so low.

CHARLES. Was Jemmy like that when you first met?

FITZROY. His family stole one of our whaleboats. I was so
    appalled by their condition that I offered to buy him for a
    single brass button. I hoped to show him a better life, that he
    might bring the same enlightenment to his people.

CHARLES. He is doing them a great service, sir.

FITZROY. High hopes on all fronts. I fear the delay to us
    beginning the surveying had quite gone to my head. I hope
    you won't begrudge me my temper.

CHARLES. I can know that you're wrong and still respect you
    for it, Captain.

FITZROY. I admire the strength of your constitution,
    Mr Darwin.

CHARLES. The weeks spent sick in my cabin tell a very
    different story.

FITZROY. You know when we first met I was inclined to reject
    your petition.

CHARLES. I didn't make much of an impression.

FITZROY. I was more concerned about the shape of your nose.

CHARLES. What's wrong with my nose?

FITZROY. I judged that it signalled weakness. Wickham! This
    doesn't look right. Turn her around and take this depth again.

CHARLES. Well, I'm glad you changed your mind, sir. And
    that the other naturalist turned the offer down.

FITZROY. You were the only candidate, Mr Darwin. One just
    needed some time to think.

The map charts the journey to the Pampas.

18.

Bones of Giants

On the open plains of the Pampas, low grasses grow over sandy soil and the Andes stand on the horizon.

An armadillo forages.

CHARLES *sneaks after it.*

It takes fright and rolls into a ball.

CHARLES *examines the creature in astonishment.*

He ties a rope around its neck then stands back to watch.

The armadillo unrolls and tries to run towards a nearby lump of earth buried in a lower strata.

CHARLES *examines the feature and reveals a giant skull.*

He uncovers a fossilised glyptodon skeleton and stands back to admire the find.

CHARLES *notices the similarity it has with the living armadillo.*

He takes notes in his journal as the world spins back to the Beagle.

19.

Tales of the Flood

On the deck of the Beagle, *the crew play with the armadillo.*

FITZROY. I leave the deck for an hour and all hell breaks lose. What is this cargo, Lieutenant?

WICKHAM. It belongs to Mr Darwin, sir.

FITZROY. Darwin! The *Beagle* has little enough room for our supplies yet you fill the hull with rocks.

CHARLES. This is a fossil, sir. Some sort of ancient creature.

MATTHEWS. The remains of a giant wiped out in the great flood. You bring us closer to the Lord, Charles.

CHARLES. Don't you think it's incredible that there are armadillo-like creatures on no other continent, and yet here in South America there have been multiple versions across the ages?

MATTHEWS. Were they not crafted by the same hand?

CHARLES. Yes, of course. After this giant perished, a similar design could have been used for the armadillo. Lyell thinks God's creation of new species is ongoing. This might be evidence for it.

FITZROY. Tell me you've started that book of yours.

CHARLES. I have, sir.

FITZROY. Then you must promise me something. Don't find another treasure until we have room to store it. Lieutenant, make arrangements to have this remarkable find shipped home.

WICKHAM. Yes, sir.

FITZROY. Keep this up, and I'll have a mind to publish your journal alongside my own record of the voyage.

A breath.

CHARLES. There's something else, Captain. If Lyell's right and the globe is always changing, there can't be a perfect place for each creation. What happens to these creatures when the world around them changes?

FITZROY. I'd say they would perish.

CHARLES. So every individual dies until the whole species is wiped out? I can't fathom that much suffering.

FITZROY. Cruelty is more common in the world than we'd like the admit. You'd have to be blind not to see that.

CHARLES. What if the great flood is just an incredible tale to explain something we don't understand?

FITZROY. I'd say it's rather more than a tale, Charles.

CHARLES. The total extermination of one of God's creations. I just can't believe that's divine.

The crew prepare to take the fossil below deck.

20.

The War of Nature

CHARLES *opens his journal and the fossil on the deck comes to life.*

The Beagle *gives way to a primeval landscape.*

The creature wanders and grazes.

CHARLES *walks with it.*

He runs his hand along its side.

Water slowly begins to flood the landscape and the fossil drowns.

A single fish swims from its skull.

It joins a larger shoal of fish.

The shoal is herded through the kelp forest by sharks.

The sharks begin to make passes at the fish.

Their strikes build into a feeding frenzy.

The map charts the journey of the Beagle *down the east coast of South America.*

21.

Jemmy's Prayer

CHARLES *sits awake late into the night, lost in thought.*
JEMMY *comes to the deck.*

CHARLES. Jemmy. Why are you still awake?

JEMMY. I have been thinking about what is to come.

CHARLES. You'll be home soon.

JEMMY. And you are such a long way away. Perhaps that is the better way to be.

CHARLES. Matthews will be with you.

JEMMY. He told me I should pray.

CHARLES. And what did you ask for?

JEMMY. For fire.

A breath.

In the south, cold is death. So Tierra del Fuego is the land of fire. It chases away the dark.

CHARLES. Then I'm sure God will provide it for you.

JEMMY. In England he is Lord.

CHARLES. Not just in England, Jemmy.

JEMMY. This place was not created by the story of the Lord. My mother told me that everything around us was made with the bodies of the gods. One of them became the moon, another took the form of the sun. When the other gods grew tired they lay down on the earth covered in their cloaks. But some of them did not wake up, and their bodies became the mountains. It was the same with all living things. We still have the heat of the gods in us. You can feel it with your fingers.

CHARLES. You can.

JEMMY. So my mother's story must be true.

A breath.

The Captain showed me England. He showed me the whole world. He made me see that all I ever knew is just one tiny part of all that is.

The deck falls away leaving them in an ocean of stars.

Two different worlds, Mr Darwin. I don't fit either any more.

The map charts the journey to Tierra del Fuego.

FITZROY. Gentlemen. We have waited long for this day, but at last it is upon us. Jemmy Button, you have been chosen by God to deliver his word to your people and so bring them into the civilised world. You walk in the footsteps of Christ our Lord, the Son of God and salvation of all mankind...

The map gives way to the shores of Tierra del Fuego.

22.

Doing God's Work

On the stony shores of Tierra del Fuego, FITZROY *addresses the crew. Great mountains loom above, covered with glaciers that groan under their own weight. The wind is high and thunder peals in the distance.*

FITZROY....I wish you well and will hold you in my prayers.

He shakes JEMMY*'s hand.*

JEMMY. Thank you, Captain.

FITZROY. Matthews. When I called for a man to accompany Mr Button, none volunteered but you. Today you farewell your life as it was, and give of yourself heart and soul to the service of these people.

MATTHEWS. I live only through God's grace and for his service.

FITZROY. True words well spoken. Go now, with faith as your strength and God as your guide you will surely build upon His holy empire.

MATTHEWS. Goodbye, Charles.

CHARLES. Farewell, my friend.

JEMMY. Safe journey home.

CHARLES. You too, Jemmy.

FITZROY. Ready the whaleboat.

The boatswain's whistle sounds the crew to stations through a roll of thunder.

CHARLES *and* FITZROY *are left alone.*

CHARLES. There's a strange feeling to this country.

FITZROY. We're on the edge of the known world, Mr Darwin.

A breath.

CHARLES. Jemmy's troubled.

FITZROY. He's our little miracle. A savage turned to Christ.

CHARLES. Why must you call him that?

FITZROY. It's what he was.

CHARLES. So because his people's ways are different to ours
we think them somehow less?

FITZROY. Through faith in Christ we bring them nearer to
God's image.

CHARLES. I'll sing the praises of missionaries as much as the
next man. But what can two men possibly achieve in a place
like this?

FITZROY. They must tame it, and through their survival we
show the strength of our faith.

CHARLES. As long as we wield rifles and the Fuegians carry
sticks, whose faith would you expect to endure?

FITZROY. Don't underestimate the worth of our cause,
Mr Darwin.

CHARLES. What are you trying to prove, sir?

A breath.

FITZROY. The last time we arrived in Tierra del Fuego,
Captain Stokes was in command of the *Beagle*. He was
struggling under the weight of his work, and when we met
with the hostility of the Fuegians he finally fell beyond our
reach. He shot himself.

Thunder peals.

The bullet lodged in his skull, and for weeks he languished in
his cabin as the rot set in. It was a long march to death, but
suicide nonetheless. A short time later I found Jemmy. I vowed
to turn him into a gentleman, to prove that no man need
despair at his place in this world because we are not born of
the same chaos. We are God's children, and by His grace, even
the lowest of men can meet a king.

FITZROY *leaves.* CHARLES *looks to the sky as the storm begins to roll over the mountains.*

The shoreline becomes the deck of the Beagle.

23.

The Land of Fire

CHARLES *works in his cabin in the early evening as* WICKHAM *keeps watch on deck.*

WICKHAM. Fire.

Points of flickering firelight appear across the coast of Tierra del Fuego.

There's fire on shore! Captain!

The coastline crawls with moving points of light.

FITZROY. What do you see?

WICKHAM. Fuegians. They carry flaming brands.

FITZROY. Hundreds of them.

CHARLES. Do you see Matthews and Jemmy?

FITZROY. On the shore.

CHARLES. We must bring them back aboard.

FITZROY. We're here to tame the locals, not flee from them.

WICKHAM. If we do not act they will perish.

CHARLES. There will be no mission if they die, sir.

WICKHAM. We can make land. There's still time. Would you permit it?

A breath.

FITZROY. Launch the whaleboat.

WICKHAM. Launch the whaleboat!

The boatswain's whistle cries.

CHARLES *joins* WICKHAM *in the whaleboat.*

FITZROY. Bring them back safely.

CHARLES. We will, sir.

WICKHAM. Let her fly.

The tiny whaleboat is thrown around by the waves.

CHARLES. I see Matthews. Toward the headland.

WICKHAM. We get any closer and we'll be torn apart in the waves.

CHARLES. Swim! Swim, Matthews! He's under the water.

They search.

There! Quickly!

WICKHAM. Take hold!

MATTHEWS *is pulled aboard.*

CHARLES. What happened?

MATTHEWS. A group of men from a neighbouring tribe arrived in the darkness. Jemmy warned me to expect them.

CHARLES. Where is he?

MATTHEWS. I didn't listen.

CHARLES. Where is he?

MATTHEWS. I couldn't find him. We must bring the crew to search.

WICKHAM. We can't, Matthews, not tonight.

Lightning rips through the sky, and CHARLES *and* WICKHAM *lean into the oars. The whaleboat returns to the* Beagle.

MATTHEWS. You must set me back ashore.

WICKHAM. We're not going to leave you to that fate.

MATTHEWS. I cannot abandon my work.

WICKHAM. Sit down, man.

MATTHEWS. I beg of you, for the sake of his soul, my soul.

WICKHAM. Sit down!

FITZROY. Matthews. Thank the Lord!

CHARLES. Get him warm.

FITZROY. Where's Jemmy?

MATTHEWS. There was such noise. The fire. They were everywhere, Robert. There was nothing else I could do.

FITZROY. He's out there by himself?

CHARLES. Jemmy knows this place better than any of us, he'll know how to survive the night.

The crew look over the burning landscape.

FITZROY. The land of fire.

Glowing embers begin to fall to deck.

WICKHAM. Boatswain, call to stations.

FITZROY. Stand down, Lieutenant.

WICKHAM. The winds are changing. We must avoid these embers.

FITZROY. The *Beagle* is not your command.

WICKHAM. No, sir, she's yours.

FITZROY. Put out the spot-fires.

WICKHAM. What are you all waiting for? She'll catch alight.

As the crew leap to action, CHARLES *comes to* MATTHEWS.

CHARLES. You can rest in my quarters. You must get warm.

MATTHEWS. No, Charles.

CHARLES. You've been through hell, Matthews. Come out of this weather.

MATTHEWS. I will not take comfort.

WICKHAM. The sails are catching!

FITZROY. Call to stations, Lieutenant. Take her towards the channel.

WICKHAM. We can't make the crossing in this weather.

FITZROY. We'll burn if we stay here.

WICKHAM. Is that your choice, Captain?

FITZROY. There is no choice, either way we are damned.

A breath.

Give the order!

WICKHAM. Towards the channel!

The boatswain's whistle cries and the crew leap to action.

FITZROY. You knew this would be a failure, Charles.

CHARLES. That's not what I said, sir.

FITZROY. Everything I promised Jemmy, it's all gone up in smoke.

CHARLES. You did exactly as you promised, sir. You brought him home.

WICKHAM. Captain! We're rounding the headland!

The swell rises as the Beagle *reaches the channel.*

Hold fast!

The crew brace themselves on the deck.

A massive wave breaks against the Beagle.

Another wave.

And another.

Wave! Wave! Wave!

A wall of water plunges the Beagle *into darkness.*

The sound rises to a crescendo.

Silence.

Interval.

24.

Rounding the Cape

In the darkness, the map charts the route to Cape Horn as the sound of a stormy sea builds, and the Beagle *is hammered by waves.*

MATTHEWS. How many are your works, Lord! In your wisdom you made them all; the earth is full of your creatures...

A wave plunges the Beagle *into darkness.*

...When you hide your face they are terrified; when you take away your breath, they die and return to the dust...

Another wave, another moment in the dark.

...When you send your spirit, they are created. You renew the face of the ground...

And another. The Beagle *begins to list dangerously.*

...May the Lord rejoice in his works...

FITZROY. She's going over.

MATTHEWS. ...He who looks at the earth and it trembles...

WICKHAM. All hands to port!

MATTHEWS. Who touches the mountains and they smoke.

The crew cling to the overturned hull of the Beagle.

Amen.

They struggle to keep hold in the swell.

They are driven underwater by another wave.

As the water recedes they lie scattered on the deck.

WICKHAM. She's righted herself.

FITZROY. A miracle. Get us out of this storm, Lieutenant.

The map charts the journey to the Falkland Islands.

25.

The Purchase of the Adventure

The Beagle *lies at anchor in the Falkland Islands as the crew make repairs.*

FITZROY *comes aboard.*

WICKHAM. Attention on deck!

FITZROY. The last few weeks have not been as we might have hoped, and our misfortunes have delayed us. I've purchased a second ship to join the *Beagle*. HMS *Adventure*. She's your command, Wickham.

WICKHAM. This wasn't in your orders, sir.

FITZROY. Yet it's necessary for us to fulfill our mandate. With two vessels we'll work twice as fast. The Admiralty will understand when we present them with perfect charts.

WICKHAM. Very good, sir.

FITZROY. As you were.

The crew scatter.

We might have lost the mission, but an accurate survey's all the Admiralty will care about.

CHARLES. Is there anything I can do to help, sir?

FITZROY. It's not your burden to bear. Spend time ashore. I'll not be any use to you.

CHARLES. You'll work it all out. I know you will.

The map charts the journey to Maldonado.

26.

The Untameable Globe

CHARLES *makes the overland journey from Maldonado to Montevideo as the map tracks his route.*

CHARLES *rejoins the* Beagle *in Montevideo.*

FITZROY. We're heading south to Tierra del Fuego. Will you join us?

CHARLES. Of course.

In Tierra del Fuego, the crew are reunited with JEMMY.

FITZROY. I'm glad to see you safe, Jemmy.

JEMMY. You too, Captain.

FITZROY. Have you told your family about your new faith?

JEMMY. They do not want to hear it, sir.

CHARLES and JEMMY *are left alone.*

They are disappointed, aren't they?

CHARLES. Not in you, Jemmy.

JEMMY. Good. I am not the one who is wrong.

The Beagle *passes through the Strait of Magellan and begins the journey north along the west coast of South America.*

FITZROY. The charts still aren't correct. I feel like I'm chasing my tail.

A breath.

I named a mountain after you, for your birthday.

CHARLES. Oh, and did you keep any geographical features for yourself?

FITZROY. Just a mountain range.

CHARLES works on the bow of the Beagle *as it continues north.*

Mount Osorno erupts in the distance.

He watches the plume of ash rise into the sky, before jumping back on to the deck.

The map charts the journey to Concepcion.

27.

The Dangers of a Lost Mind

The Beagle *lies at anchor near Concepción, which has been ravaged by the effects of an earthquake.*

CHARLES. The whole town's in ruins. I can't see the sense in it.

WICKHAM. Maybe there is none.

CHARLES. The volcano we saw coming up the coast. It must be related somehow. Surely it can't have been a coincidence.

WICKHAM. Perhaps we should call it God?

The tremor of an earthquake shakes the Beagle.

CHARLES. Another earthquake.

FITZROY *comes to the deck.*

FITZROY. It seems that wherever we have sailed these past months, we are met with destruction.

A breath.

Wickham. How fares HMS *Adventure*?

WICKHAM. Well, sir.

FITZROY. What would you say to us returning to Tierra del Fuego to check measurements once more?

WICKHAM. It isn't necessary, sir. There are only minor inconsistencies in the charts.

FITZROY. Perhaps you're right. And not alone in your opinion.

FITZROY produces an opened letter.

WICKHAM. What's this?

FITZROY. A letter from the Admiralty, admonishing me for the purchase of the *Adventure* and questioning the ever-increasing length of our voyage.

WICKHAM reads.

What were your orders, Wickham, if I should fail in my task?

WICKHAM. You haven't failed at anything, sir.

FITZROY. Tell me.

WICKHAM. The same as yours last time. To return the *Beagle* to England by the most direct route.

FITZROY hands WICKHAM his hat.

FITZROY. The *Beagle* is yours.

CHARLES. No! You can't.

WICKHAM. You'll be court-martialled, sir.

FITZROY. So be it. We've been given a clear message.

MATTHEWS. FitzRoy's right. All important things are lost.

CHARLES. The loss of the Christian mission is not reason to throw everything away.

FITZROY. I had one chance to atone for my Captain, to prove that nothing is so wicked in this world that it might drive a man to such ends. I was wrong, Charles.

CHARLES. His mistakes are not yours, Robert.

FITZROY. Yet history finds a way of repeating itself.

CHARLES. You're not in your right mind.

FITZROY. Exactly.

FITZROY leaves.

CHARLES. The voyage cannot end like this.

WICKHAM. It already has, Charles.

CHARLES. Is there really an issue with the charts?

WICKHAM. Nothing anyone but FitzRoy would care about.

CHARLES. It's madness.

WICKHAM. We reach the edge of our understanding, and all things fall to dust.

CHARLES. He needs to see the worth of our work. What we might still achieve together.

WICKHAM. You'll have a hard time convincing him of that.

CHARLES. We must find something to restore his faith.

WICKHAM. My orders are clear.

CHARLES. I know I can make sense of what we've seen. Earthquakes, a volcano, they're the forces that Lyell thinks reshape the earth.

A breath.

WICKHAM. You'll learn nothing from the deck of the *Beagle*.

CHARLES. No.

WICKHAM. How soon can you be ready to land?

CHARLES. What about your orders?

WICKHAM. There are preparations to be made before we can leave. Extensive preparations. I think it's most likely to take some weeks.

CHARLES. Thank you, Wickham.

WICKHAM. One chance, Charles, that's all I can give you.

CHARLES. That's all I need.

The ground rumbles again, and the Beagle *gives way to a rocky shoreline.*

28.

Slow Change on an Ancient Earth

On the shore, marine life has been lifted out of the water by the earthquake.

CHARLES *picks up a shell and examines it.*

There is an aftershock and the ground lifts again.

CHARLES *pockets the shell and moves on.*

WICKHAM *stands on the deck of the* Beagle *with* FITZROY*'s hat in his hand.*

CHARLES *climbs a steep mountain peak.*

He reaches the top. It's cloaked in cloud.

CHARLES *looks around him as the ground groans under the pressure of the breaking fault line.*

He brushes away some rubble and reveals a fossil.

CHARLES. A fossilised seashell.

CHARLES *looks around him.*

Thousands of them. This land was beneath the ocean.

CHARLES *writes in his journal as the world turns beneath him.*

The stars come out.

He is bathed in the light of his epiphany.

CHARLES *begins his descent, and the mountain becomes the* Beagle.

29.

Small Things, and Something Greater

CHARLES *climbs aboard the* Beagle *and meets* WICKHAM *on deck.*

CHARLES. Small things can change the world, Wickham. It's past time we trusted in that.

   CHARLES *gives him the fossil and knocks on the door of* FITZROY'*s cabin.*

WICKHAM. You're mad.

   FITZROY *comes to the deck.*

FITZROY. It's a bold move to leave a ship when her commander has direct orders to sail.

CHARLES. A bold move was necessary.

FITZROY. And was your foray worth the risk?

CHARLES. That's your choice.

   He hands FITZROY *the shell.*

FITZROY. A seashell?

CHARLES. From a rock pool lifted out of the water by earthquakes. And this.

   WICKHAM *hands* FITZROY *the fossil.*

   From the top of the Andes.

   FITZROY *examines them.*

   Earthquakes can raise mountains. This is proof of it.

FITZROY. Then you have your great find to take home.

CHARLES. Lyell was right, sir. What if he's also correct about the ongoing creation of new life?

FITZROY. That would be proof of God.

   A breath.

   Could you find such a thing?

CHARLES. Not if we go home.

A breath.

FITZROY. Wickham. Seems I might have made a rash decision. I wonder if it would spare us both some embarrassment if the ship's log were edited.

WICKHAM. Will you give me your word we won't head south again?

FITZROY. I don't see why we'd need to.

WICKHAM. Then there's nothing to edit, sir.

FITZROY. Good man. We've new charts to draw and measurements to be taken. We're going home the long way around. Set a course to the Galápagos Islands.

WICKHAM. Boatswain!

CHARLES. Have you been to the islands before?

FITZROY. I only know them by reputation.

CHARLES. And what's that?

FITZROY. The sea around the archipelago is a maze of deadly currents. The land is rugged, sun-scorched, and almost uncrossable.

CHARLES. That sounds thoroughly uninviting.

FITZROY. Don't you think for one second we're going there for your benefit.

The world spins beneath the Beagle *as the map charts the journey to the Galápagos archipelago.*

30.

The Galápagos

A sea-lion pup plays in the waves as they crash against the shore of one of the Galápagos Islands.

A marine iguana dives into the water to feed on algae growing from a rock.

Tiny fish eat the sediment it disturbs.

The fish are chased by a flightless cormorant.

One of the fish is caught by a blue-footed booby as it dives into the water.

CHARLES *watches from the rocky shoreline as the booby surfaces and takes flight.*

The iguana comes to shore to bask in the sun.

CHARLES *approaches and it snorts salt in his face.*

He is joined by a sea-lion pup.

It is playful, but when CHARLES *reaches to touch it, it dives back into the water and out of reach.*

CHARLES *sees another blue-footed booby perched above him and climbs to it.*

The booby takes flight.

The world spins as he watches it soar over the islands.

Higher on the slopes, CHARLES *is interrupted by a flock of tiny finches.*

One of them lands on his boot and he kicks it away.

It lands on his shoulder, and is joined by another.

CHARLES *swats them both away.*

The entire flock land on him and start to pick at his clothes and hair.

He shakes them off.

There is a deep breath in the distance.

The finches fly towards the sound.

A giant tortoise eats in the grass.

The birds flit around it, catching the insects that it disturbs.

CHARLES *is awestruck by the creature.*

He moves towards it.

The tortoise hisses loudly and pulls its head into its shell.

CHARLES *gathers some of the foliage it was eating and coaxes it out.*

The tortoise eats the foliage CHARLES *sets before it.*

He tries to touch it, but it swings its head to keep clear.

CHARLES *picks up the foliage and the tortoise becomes interested in him.*

He leads it into the open.

The sun begins to set.

CHARLES *admires the tortoise in the fading light.*

He leads it aboard the Beagle.

31.

Darwin's Ark

The inside of the Beagle*'s hull is littered with specimens.*
FITZROY *watches* CHARLES *work.*

FITZROY. You're turning my ship into quite an ark.

CHARLES. They're all the most curious creatures, Robert.

FITZROY. Perfectly created for curious islands.

CHARLES. There's no doubt it's new land. Not long ago there would have been nothing but ocean here.

FITZROY. They were recently populated then?

CHARLES. Must have been. But the creatures all bear remarkable similarities to those of the continent. I think they might have been castaways.

FITZROY. You're saying a two hundred-pound-tortoise somehow made its way across five hundred miles of open ocean?

CHARLES. There are so many riddles I can't explain. This iguana feeds at sea. Its cousin in the Amazon lives entirely on land. Perhaps it learnt to swim. But that can't explain the shrunken wings of the cormorants. Why would God create such creatures?

FITZROY. Man desires dogs and pigeons in all number of fancy varieties, why should the Lord not be afforded the same want?

CHARLES. There's more. The locals knew which island these tortoises came from just by the shape of their shells. It's the same with the species of mockingbird. Only slight differences from one another, but marked.

FITZROY. I'm sure you'll find the sense in it.

CHARLES. Why would God put such creative energy into minutely changing the appearance of animals on such tiny islands?

FITZROY. Because He populates His creation as He sees fit, and that is the way of it.

CHARLES. I know that.

FITZROY. Then acknowledge it.

CHARLES. I can't. Not yet.

FITZROY. Why not?

CHARLES. If you send a trained naturalist into the field, every new discovery will reassure him of what he already thinks he knows. Send a young man who knows nothing and there's no telling what he might find.

FITZROY. Who said that?

CHARLES. Someone much wiser than me.

FITZROY. Curiosity for its own sake is not wisdom, Charles.

CHARLES. I need to work.

FITZROY *leaves* CHARLES *alone in his cabin.*

32.

The Mysterious Tongue of the Wilderness

CHARLES *sits with the creatures late into the night as the* Beagle *charts a course into the Pacific Ocean.*

He turns the fossil from the Andes over and over in his hands.

He holds food above the tortoises.

The saddleback tortoise can reach, the dome tortoise cannot.

CHARLES *collects his journal and goes to sit in the bow.*

As he thinks, the point of light appears and dances in the night sky.

A dome tortoise wanders the cosmos.

Its shell becomes a horizon.

Earthquakes raise the ground.

The new peak is the raised shell of a saddleback tortoise.

A cormorant soars through the air above it.

Its wing becomes a peninsula.

The ocean wears the wing down.

The shrunken wing belongs to a cormorant that soars beneath the waves.

Volcanoes push land out of the ocean.

They become the raised scales of an iguana.

The eye of the iguana becomes the Earth.

The Earth becomes the point of light.

The point of light begins to draw the tree of life.

Before it fully forms, the tree is lost in the chaos of its own blinding light.

CHARLES *slams his journal closed and climbs back to the deck.*

33.

An Unreachable Horizon

The Beagle *makes her way through the Pacific Ocean on a quiet night.*

CHARLES. Matthews? Your skin is blistered.

MATTHEWS. It is only worldly pain.

CHARLES. Have you not left the deck?

MATTHEWS. I cannot rest, Charles.

CHARLES. When we were first aboard you told me it would take time to understand the value of my work.

MATTHEWS. We were fools caught up in the beginning of things.

CHARLES. No, you were right. I would say the same thing to you now.

MATTHEWS. I had one task. To bring the light of Christianity to Jemmy and his people, and save them from eternal damnation.

CHARLES. What happened in Tierra del Fuego was not your fault.

MATTHEWS. Do you think God was punishing us?

CHARLES. You mean the power of the storm? I don't think that was God. It was just the way of the Earth.

MATTHEWS. How mighty is the power of nature, that it might replace the hand of the Lord?

CHARLES. Beyond anything we could ever comprehend. It might somehow be the source of new life.

MATTHEWS. You speak such terrible words.

CHARLES. I mean them as a comfort.

MATTHEWS. Is God here with us now, do you think?

CHARLES. I don't know any more.

MATTHEWS. I promised myself, I would sit on this deck until I found the Lord again. Until I felt His grace.

CHARLES. Perhaps you don't need to find it.

MATTHEWS. The only thing that elevates mankind from the animals is our knowledge that there is something more, something greater than us. Without that we are nothing more than dust.

CHARLES. I know that.

MATTHEWS. Yet if what you have said were true, there would be only endless waves and an unreachable horizon.

CHARLES. That's not what I meant.

MATTHEWS. I could never accept such a world, Charles. And neither should you.

   MATTHEWS *leaves* CHARLES *alone on deck.*

   The Beagle *continues her journey to New Zealand.*

34.

A Different Kind of Savage

The crew gather to say farewell to MATTHEWS *near Kaitaia, New Zealand.*

MATTHEWS. My brother's mission is close. By his account the Maori have taken to the word of Christ more keenly than the Fuegians.

FITZROY. Are you sure this is what you want?

MATTHEWS. God's work is never finished, Robert.

FITZROY. I wish you the best, my friend.

MATTHEWS. Keep an eye on your naturalist. It's not just savages that need our guidance.

The world spins, and the Beagle *makes her way to Sydney.*

35.

A Plague of Thought

CHARLES *watches a platypus forage in an Australian creek.*

FITZROY. Another strange creature.

CHARLES. This land is full of them. A fool might be forgiven for thinking that there were two distinct creators.

FITZROY. You're not a fool though, are you?

CHARLES. There's an ant lion here that's just the same as those in England. No two craftsmen could ever hit on such an artificial contrivance.

FITZROY. How would you explain that fellow?

CHARLES. Beaks, and fins, and fur are found throughout all the animal kingdom.

FITZROY. They are.

CHARLES. Proof that one hand has worked across the whole of creation. It cannot be any other way.

FITZROY. A wise thought.

CHARLES. My first for a while.

A breath.

FITZROY. Matthews was worried for you. What did you say to him?

CHARLES. The wilderness has a mysterious tongue. It teaches awful doubt.

FITZROY. What did you say?

CHARLES. I can't tell you.

FITZROY. Why not? Charles? What did you say?

A breath.

CHARLES. What would it mean for the world, Robert, if we were to lose God?

FITZROY. There's no answer to that question.

CHARLES. No, and only a fool would ask it. I'll keep on with the geology and we can leave it at that.

The world spins and the map charts the Beagle*'s journey to Keeling Island.*

36.

The Wisdom of Coral

The Beagle *lies at anchor in the lagoon of Keeling Island as* CHARLES *packs specimens away.*

WICKHAM. What are you doing holed up in your cabin?

CHARLES. I've seen enough islands to last me a lifetime.

WICKHAM. Every mile from here brings us closer to home.

CHARLES. I never thought I'd be excited to see England again. What are we going to find waiting for us?

WICKHAM. How about that young lass you were telling me about?

CHARLES. I promised her I'd make something more of myself. Five years, and all I'll have to show for it are beetles.

WICKHAM. You've got some pretty interesting rocks too. Assuming she fancies that sort of thing.

CHARLES. She doesn't.

WICKHAM. So it's the priesthood for you after all?

CHARLES. I've seen far too much for that.

WICKHAM. You're still not satisfied though, are you?

CHARLES. I just thought, for a moment, I might be on to something else. Something incredible. Got carried away with myself.

WICKHAM. You're not the only one.

CHARLES. You'd think after all we've been through I would have learnt the dangers of dreaming too big.

WICKHAM. I thought you said it was small things that change the world?

CHARLES. That was my professor's mantra, it suited me perfectly because I thought the whole world too big to fathom. But the things it led me to were totally beyond me.

WICKHAM. I don't believe that for a second.

CHARLES. There's no place in the civilised world for some of the thoughts I've had.

WICKHAM. Lucky we're not in the civilised world then.

CHARLES. If I speak out, I'll damn myself and everyone around me.

WICKHAM. Do you think FitzRoy would have brought you this far if he thought you were a danger? He believed in you. We all did.

CHARLES. He won't like what I've got to say.

WICKHAM. That's never been a problem in the past.

CHARLES. The words are a plague. I know the consequence of them spreading and I will not suffer it to pass.

WICKHAM. I can't fathom how anything that you've done could possibly be so terrible.

CHARLES. Well it is, and most definitely not worth the toll it would take.

WICKHAM. That's just life. It's nothing without its challenges.

CHARLES. If you knew what I know you would not push this further.

WICKHAM. Listen to me, Charles. It makes no sense that this island should survive the barrage of the waves, yet it's made even more magnificent by the struggle.

CHARLES. That's not by chance.

WICKHAM. Care to enlighten me?

CHARLES. Living mounds of coral skirt the lagoon. Whatever damage a storm might cause is repaired by the work of a million tiny architects.

WICKHAM. It sounds like there's wisdom to be found in coral.

A breath.

CHARLES. God save me, John Wickham. I'm a fool who cannot help himself.

WICKHAM. You'd be more of a fool if you could. We dock in South Africa before we head north to Europe.

CHARLES. South Africa?

WICKHAM. Cape Town, make your time there count for something, for God's sake.

WICKHAM *leaves* CHARLES *alone on deck.*

CHARLES *looks into the water and watches a green sea turtle being cleaned by fish.*

The turtle begins to swim.

The map charts the Beagle*'s journey to the southern most tip of the African continent.*

37.

On the Cape of Good Hope

CHARLES *approaches a small house tucked into the slopes of Table Mountain.*

He is met by a wizened old man hurrying to leave.

CHARLES. Excuse me, sir.

A blink.

Might I have a moment?

HERSCHEL. You spend your life looking into the heavens and a moment is not a long time. Yet you find me in a moment I do not have to spare. Goodnight to you.

CHARLES. Please, sir.

HERSCHEL. A boat has docked, there's someone I must meet.

CHARLES. What's her name?

HERSCHEL. It's a he.

CHARLES. The boat?

HERSCHEL. The *Beagle*.

CHARLES. The *Beagle*'s a ship, sir.

HERSCHEL. You know it?

CHARLES. Very well.

HERSCHEL. Do you by chance also know a young man named Darwin? He was the pupil of a dear friend of mine from Cambridge.

CHARLES. I haven't seen Professor Henslow for very long time.

A breath.

HERSCHEL. Mr Darwin! Henslow thinks the world of you, young man.

CHARLES. He was constantly speaking of your work.

HERSCHEL. Was he just? Come! Come!

CHARLES. I always dreamt of having an adventure just like one of yours.

HERSCHEL. A voyage is a rare gift. By all accounts you are so driven by your passion, so full of life.

CHARLES. Before I left England I had no idea what the world was really like.

HERSCHEL. Neither did I.

CHARLES. Since then I've found bones from ancient giants, felt the crust of the earth move beneath my feet. I've seen mountains being built, and walked on islands newly grown from the ocean.

HERSCHEL. It sounds like you've read Lyell.

CHARLES. I've lived it, sir. I can hardly see the world in any way other than through his eyes.

HERSCHEL. He'll be delighted to hear as much.

CHARLES. It's one thing to see the perfect answer to a question. Another entirely to be met with a new riddle.

HERSCHEL. That is progress, Mr Darwin.

CHARLES. I have a terrible feeling I might have seen too much.

HERSCHEL. Try me.

CHARLES. In every place we've travelled, I've been met with the most remarkable creatures, each perfectly suited to their station.

HERSCHEL. Go on.

CHARLES. There are thoughts knitting themselves together in my mind that the creation of new species might somehow be a natural process.

HERSCHEL. Now that is radical.

A breath.

The transmutation of species. You're not the first to have had such thoughts.

CHARLES. What if there were a mechanism to be found?

HERSCHEL. If you could explain it? Now there's a notion that would have the clergy shaking in their boots.

CHARLES. I'm not the sort to start a revolution. I know the importance of faith.

HERSCHEL. Are you worried about faith, or religion.

CHARLES. They are the same thing.

HERSCHEL. No, young man, they are not. Religion is a dogma used by men to prescribe for others how they must view the world. Faith, however – do you believe in the truth of what you've found?

CHARLES. I cannot doubt it if I try.

HERSCHEL. Then you must have faith in that.

CHARLES. And where would that leave God?

HERSCHEL. We understand the process whereby a child is conceived and brought into the world, yet we still call it a miracle, a gift from above, if you will. How is this any different?

CHARLES. My thoughts wouldn't be welcome.

HERSCHEL. Few enlightened ideas ever are, Mr Darwin. Build it carefully, from a million observations, and if your theory is fit, it will survive.

CHARLES. My theory? You think it could be worthy of that?

HERSCHEL. It's not a question of worth, young man. Not yet. You are talking about a work that will take a lifetime.

CHARLES. That's exactly what I need.

HERSCHEL. It's what we all need. Speaking of…

He pulls a leather-wrapped package from his cloak.

Give this to Henslow for me.

CHARLES *takes the package.*

Take a look.

CHARLES *unwraps the package to reveal an image of* HERSCHEL*'s face on a glass slate.*

I call it a photo-graph.

Light, captured on glass, to paint a picture.

CHARLES. It's not impossible.

HERSCHEL. Very nearly. But given enough time, I tend to think there are very few things that truly are.

The light from the photograph plays on CHARLES*'s face as Table Mountain spins away.*

The Beagle *begins her journey north along the western coast of Africa.*

38.

Doubts as to the Fixity of Species

The Beagle *draws near to England.*

CHARLES. I owe you a debt for what you've given me.

FITZROY. Your board was fully paid.

CHARLES. You took me on as a nobody, now you're bringing me home with memories I would never have dreamt might be mine.

FITZROY. I'm glad you've found the voyage worthy of your time.

CHARLES. Beyond anything I'd ever hoped for. Collecting beetles in England certainly didn't prepare me for the sheer breadth of creation.

A breath.

Back in the Americas you told me you had a mind to publish my journal, alongside your own records.

FITZROY. A lot has happened since then.

CHARLES. This is it, Robert. My contribution to the voyage. If you'll have it.

FITZROY *takes the journal.*

It's a marvel really, everything we've seen. How each creature perfectly suits its home, even though the land is constantly changing.

FITZROY. The power of the Lord knows no limits.

CHARLES. Neither does the imagination of man.

FITZROY. What's that supposed to mean?

CHARLES. Do you remember the giant fossil from the Pampas and how similar it was to the armadillo?

FITZROY. Yes, of course.

CHARLES. And in the Galápagos, I found the creatures that were so alike to those of the Americas that I thought they must have been castaways.

FITZROY. You said yourself they were different to those of the continent.

CHARLES. I did. But I think that might have been because they'd changed.

FITZROY. An animal cannot alter its form, Charles, they are now as they were first created.

CHARLES. Can we really believe that each species springs into being from nothing?

FITZROY. Is this the nonsense you fed to Matthews?

CHARLES. If we can accept that natural laws govern the oceans, and the mountains, even the objects in the heavens, it just has to be the case for living things as well.

FITZROY. Would you have this to be true of all creatures?

CHARLES. I don't know yet. There's still years of work to do.

FITZROY. Then what of man?

CHARLES. If life is all one great tree, it would only make sense for us to have our own branch.

FITZROY. You would reduce all of mankind to savages.

CHARLES. There's no such thing. The world is so much more complex than we know.

FITZROY. You speak of chaos, Charles, as though the whole of creation were somehow there by chance rather than design.

CHARLES. No, there will be a perfect order to it, and I'll work out what it is.

FITZROY. Either you work for the glory of God and the good of mankind, or you should not work at all.

CHARLES. If a million small changes can reshape the Earth, then why not an animal?

FITZROY. Because they are not the same in God's eyes.

CHARLES. Says who?

FITZROY. All sensible men.

CHARLES. Most sensible men have never travelled beyond the borders of their county, have never seen more than a handful of landscapes or species. How can such a man possibly tell us of creation when he is so obviously ignorant of the real wonder of the wider earth?

A breath.

The hand of nature and the hand of God. Robert, they're the same thing.

FITZROY. The *Beagle* will not be remembered for your lunacy.

CHARLES. No. That's my burden. But this, we did this together. Read it, at least, and then we'll go our separate ways.

FITZROY takes the journal from him. Arctic terns fly in the air above CHARLES's head as the map charts his journey home.

39.

The Company of Dreamers

Back at The Mount, CHARLES watches his father in the early-morning light.

ROBERT. Charles?

CHARLES. Good morning, Father.

ROBERT. Where in God's name did you come from?

CHARLES. I arrived late last night. Didn't want to wake you.

ROBERT. You little rat.

CHARLES. I have so much to tell you.

ROBERT. My boy has come home!

HENSLOW enters.

HENSLOW. What's this?

CHARLES. Professor! What on earth are you doing here?

HENSLOW. I was there to send you on your way, seemed a shame not to welcome you home. How was it, my young friend?

CHARLES. Better than you could ever imagine. You've seen everything I sent home?

HENSLOW. Yes. And so have a good many others.

CHARLES. What do you mean?

HENSLOW. You'll have to forgive this old man for a couple of published excerpts, and a few specimens on display.

CHARLES. Professor! None of it was ready!

HENSLOW. And yet everyone wants a piece of the most promising young naturalist of the century! You've caused quite the stir, my young friend.

ROBERT. Apparently you are so very clever.

CHARLES. It's so good to be home.

HENSLOW. Don't go hanging up your boots yet, Charles. You have to get yourself to London. All the bigwigs want to see you. Even Lyell and his lot want an audience.

CHARLES. The Charles Lyell?

HENSLOW. The very same. They'll all be eager to read the rest of your notes.

CHARLES. Well, they'll have to wait. I left my journal with FitzRoy.

HENSLOW. Why in heaven's name did you do that?

CHARLES. I owed him the first read.

HENSLOW. Well then, let's just pray he likes it.

CHARLES. There's something far more important. Although it's just a thought.

HENSLOW. This had better be a mighty thought.

CHARLES. I think it might take a lifetime to understand.

HENSLOW. What more could we have asked for?

A breath.

CHARLES. It doesn't sound like I'm going to have the time to complete my theology training, Father.

ROBERT. That certainly seems to be the case.

CHARLES. I'll pay my own way. I need nothing more than your good grace.

ROBERT. How your head is utterly changed. You shall have an allowance, as large and for as long as you need. My son, the gentleman naturalist.

CHARLES produces the leather-wrapped package.

CHARLES. I met Herschel in Cape Town. He sent this for you, Professor.

HENSLOW reveals the glass slate.

It's not impossible.

HENSLOW. How blessed am I to know the company of dreamers.

A breath.

CHARLES. May I borrow a horse, Father? I need to see Emma.

ROBERT. She's here, Charles.

CHARLES. In Shrewsbury?

ROBERT. The Mount. She arrived the day we heard you'd docked, must have stepped out for a walk.

CHARLES. Excuse me, Professor.

HENSLOW. Of course my boy. There are a few things in this world that are more important than lofty thoughts.

ROBERT. Remember you've been gone a long time, son.

CHARLES. I know where to find her.

The courtyard of The Mount gives way to the countryside outside Shrewsbury.

40.

Ending at the Beginning

CHARLES *finishes his story for* EMMA *in the late afternoon.*

CHARLES. That's it. All of it. The whole voyage. All I can remember.

A breath.

What do you think?

EMMA. It's quite a tale. But you've gone and missed the most important part.

CHARLES. There's no more to it.

EMMA. What about the end?

A breath.

CHARLES. All right… after all that time away I stood right here, looking at my oldest friend, and I thought that everything was as it should be.

EMMA. Go on.

CHARLES. But you said I was gone too long.

EMMA. You were.

CHARLES. That too much time had passed.

EMMA. It had.

CHARLES. You said you were engaged.

EMMA. I never said those words, Mr Darwin.

CHARLES. You told me you were spoken for.

EMMA. I thought you had an eye for detail?

CHARLES. You received a proposal.

EMMA. I did. Though it was done rather poorly. On this hill, five years ago.

A breath.

CHARLES. That was me.

EMMA. That was you.

CHARLES. There's no one else?

EMMA. Not a soul.

A breath.

You've just told me the most remarkable story. A tale of forests, oceans and volcanos. And a terrifying thought you didn't want to bring home.

CHARLES. But you listened. You did not turn away.

EMMA. Because it wasn't a tale of grand deeds. It was an honest one. Of small things. Of how the world is ever more remarkable for the parts that make it whole. Of exactly who I hoped would come home to me.

A kiss.

CHARLES. I'm sorry I was gone so long.

EMMA. The most important things take time, Charles. We won abolishment. Slavery is illegal across the entire reaches of the empire.

CHARLES. You changed the world without ever leaving home. There's a lesson in that.

EMMA. It seems both of our affairs are quite in order. Except for this.

She hands the paper-wrapped package to him.

CHARLES. For Charles Darwin. You have my thanks for all that you have done, and my blessing to do as you will. I can know that you're wrong, and still respect you for it. Captain Robert FitzRoy.

A breath.

EMMA. I loosened it for you.

CHARLES *slowly unwraps the package, and pulls his journal from the paper.*

CHARLES. My journal. This is all of it. Every last detail.

A breath.

EMMA. You are going to meet an even greater challenge.

CHARLES. This is just the beginning.

EMMA. Then we'll face it together.

CHARLES *opens the journal and they are bathed in its light.*

CHARLES (*voice-over*). When I view all beings not as special creations, but as the descendants of other beings, they seem to me to become ennobled.

The young couple are lost in the darkness.

The glowing sphere appears and draws the tree of life in the cosmos.

There is grandeur in this view of life, with its several powers, having been originally breathed by the Creator into a few forms, or into one.

The crew of the Beagle *sail below.*

And that whilst this planet has gone cycling on according to the fixed laws of nature, from so simple a beginning, endless forms most beautiful and most wonderful have been, and are being, evolved.

The Beagle *moves on.*

The sphere splits in two.

Black.

The End.

www.nickhernbooks.co.uk

facebook.com/nickhernbooks

twitter.com/nickhernbooks